Ticklemonster and me

A Play-Along Book • by Max Haynes

A Doubleday Book for Young Readers

For Tookie,
the original Ticklemonster

A NOTE TO PARENTS

Ticklemonster and Me isn't your usual picture book. Here *two* stories take place at once. And you and your child are the stars of both! As Tough Teddy's adventure unfolds on the right-hand pages, you can act it out with your son or daughter. The boy and his mom pictured on the left-hand pages will show you how to do it. All you'll need are a bed or couch, a blanket, and a sense of humor—this is a book *full of giggles*!

Before you read *Ticklemonster and Me* with your child, you should explain the book's format. Point out the left-hand hints: "See how the boy and his mom are bouncing on the bed on page eight? That's a hint that we can play along with the story by doing our *own* bouncing." Your child will quickly embrace the game and will likely even expand on the action. Don't be surprised if your child is still pretending to be Tough Teddy long after you close this book.

Ticklemonster and Me was created to inspire imaginative play. Encourage your child to branch off from this Teddy-and-Ticklemonster story into new episodes. Ask your child if he or she would like to tell *you* a story about Tough Teddy. And if you have more than one child, feel free to add another character to the story: Maybe Rough and Tough Teddy are twins! This is a book meant to be adapted freely.

Be sure to try the extra tickle games at the end of the book. These too will likely put new, playful ideas in your child's head.

Is your child ready to laugh out loud? Ready to be tickled? Then *play along*!

Max

Once there was a little bear (who was a lot like you), and his name was Tough Teddy. He liked to walk around the woods gritting his teeth and making scary faces. *Grrrrr!* He wasn't afraid of anything . . . *except* being tickled.

Tough Teddy was so brave that he wasn't afraid to
camp out in the deep dark woods all by himself.
But just in case there was some sort of a ticklemonster
hiding nearby, he made a nice big tent.

Now it just so happened that very close by, there was a huge *something* thumping around in the bushes. *Thump. Bump. Thump. Bump.* What could it be?

Oh no! It was a ticklemonster! And on its face was a big red nose for smelling teddy bears. It snuffled and snorted and got closer and closer until . . .

"Aha! I've got you!" yelled the ticklemonster.

Ticklemonster grabbed the sides of the tent and flapped it up and down until it fell to the ground. There was Tough Teddy with no place to hide. *Uh-ohhh.*

Then Ticklemonster did what ticklemonsters do best . . .
it tickled!
First it tickled Tough Teddy's feet. *Tickle, tickle, tickle.*

Then it tickled Tough Teddy's ribs. *Tickle, tickle, tickle.*
But all of a sudden it stopped . . .

. . . so it could tickle Tough Teddy's chin.
Tickle, tickle, tickle, tickle, tickle.

Then it tickled all the tickle places at the same time.
Tough Teddy thought he might die laughing!
He had to think of a way to stop Ticklemonster.
Suddenly he remembered what teddy bears do best.

He grabbed the ticklemonster and gave it a *great big* BEAR HUG. "Ooof!" said the ticklemonster. Tough Teddy squeezed the ticklemonster *so* hard . . .

. . . that the ticklemonster melted into a
big puddle of mush!
Now Ticklemonster will *never* bother anyone *ever* again.
Never . . . ever . . . *ever* . . .

MORE TICKLE GAMES

Parents: There are unlimited ways to surprise and amuse your child through tickle-game playing. Here are four of the author's favorites for you to try.

Hog Slobber

This is another playacting game. Pretend you're a very hungry pig. Say "Where's my supper?" as your snout sniffs closer and closer to your child's neck. Really ham it up! Then when you are in tickle range, start snuffling and snorting: You're a hog who's found his dinner slop. Watch how quickly your child starts to squeal!

Dirty Foot

For this game, your child must be barefoot. Fool the child by asking "What's that on the bottom of your foot?" Pretend there really is something strange there. Look concerned, or confused, or disgusted. Make all sorts of funny faces. While saying "Here, I'll get it off for you," hold the child's ankle and, pretending to scratch something away from the foot, tickle tickle tickle!

Creep Mouse

Creep Mouse is a classic tickle game. Your parents may have played it with you. While walking your fingers up your child's arm, recite or sing the following: "Creep mouse, creep mouse, from the barn to the house, from the house to the kitchen, from the kitchen to the cupboard, from the cupboard to the CHEESE!" As you say "CHEESE!" your fingers should reach the child's chin. Tickle away!

Hand Language

Not just a tickle game, Hand Language also explores the concept of unspoken communication. First, ask your child, "How do you say 'Quiet, please' with your hand?" Next ask, "How do you say 'Good-bye' with your hand?" Then, "How do you say 'Okay' with your hand?" Finally, "When your teacher asks a question, how do you say 'I know' with your hand?" And—you guessed it!—when the child raises his or her hand, give that exposed armpit a good tickle!

A Doubleday Book for Young Readers

Published by Bantam Doubleday Dell Publishing Group, Inc.
1540 Broadway, New York, NY 10036

Doubleday and the portrayal of an anchor with a dolphin are trademarks of
Bantam Doubleday Dell Publishing Group, Inc.

Library of Congress Cataloging-in-Publication Data

Haynes, Max.
Ticklemonster and Me / by Max Haynes.   p.   cm.
"A play-along book." Summary: Illustrations present a story about how Tough Teddy turns
the tables on the Ticklemonster while those on facing pages show parents and children how to
act out the story. Includes directions for other tickling games.
ISBN 0-385-32582-7   [1. Tickling—Fiction.]   I. Title.
PZ7.H3149149Ti   1999 [E]—dc21   97-40850   CIP   AC

The text of this book is set in 49-point Trixie Bold.
Book design by Max Haynes and Semadar Megged
Manufactured in the United States of America
April 1999
10 9 8 7 6 5 4 3 2 1